WILLIAM'S W WELLINGTONS

William and the Genie

BBC CHILDREN'S BOOKS

One evening, William's mother was reading William a bedtime story. It was all about a king who stole a genie's magic lamp.

"Time to go to sleep now," said William's mum. "I'll finish the story tomorrow."

"How can I go to sleep?" thought William. "I need to find out what happens to the poor genie without his magic lamp."

Then William remembered his magic wish
wellingtons.

"I know! I'll go and find the genie and see what
happens myself," said William. He put on his
wellingtons and made a wish.

Suddenly, William found himself flying through the sky.

"This flying quilt is just as good as a magic carpet," laughed William.

Before long, William arrived at a mysterious cave. He headed for the big, gaping mouth and flew straight in.

It was very dark and eerie inside the cave.
"I wonder where the genie is," said William.

"I'm stuck up here," called a miserable voice. "I've lost my lamp and I've nowhere else to go."

"Don't worry," said William. "I'll help you!"
"What can you do?" cried the genie.

"I've got a pair of magic wish wellingtons," said William, proudly. "They can make wishes come true."

"Can you wish for a lamp for me to live in?" asked the genie, hopefully.

"That's easy!" said William. He wished as hard as he could.

A bedside lamp appeared.

"I don't want that sort of lamp," grumbled the genie.

William wished again. Suddenly a huge street lamp sprouted up with the poor genie stuck inside it! "Get me out of here!" shouted the genie, crossly.

William made another wish, but this time the genie appeared inside a light bulb. He looked rather upset.

"Maybe you should choose your own lamp,"
suggested William, making another wish. Hundreds
of different lamps appeared all round the cave.

"Oh, no, I don't want any of those," said the genie, in despair. "All I want is my old lamp back again."

"The King has got that," said William. "Let's fly to his palace and see if we can get it."

"It's far too dangerous," wailed the genie as they flew along. "As soon as it gets dark the King gets into a terrible temper. He'll probably put us in prison."

Outside the door of the palace stood a fierce-looking guard.

"Watch out! He'll see us!" whispered the genie.

William had a good idea. He made a wish and a monkey appeared. It started to make rude faces at the guard.

The guard chased after it and William and the
genie slipped quickly into the palace.

Inside the palace William and the genie could hear the King shouting angrily in his bedroom.

William and the genie peered nervously round the
door.

They could see that the King was trying to read a book in bed, but something was bothering him.

"That's my lamp!" whispered the genie, spotting it on the King's bedside table. "But how can we get it back?"

William bravely leapt up on to the King's bed.
"What's wrong, your Majesty?" he asked.
"It's this lamp," grumbled the King. "It doesn't
make enough light for me to read my book."

William made a wish with his magic wish wellingtons . . .

. . . and a smart bedside lamp appeared.

"Would you swap your lamp for this lovely new one?" asked William.

The King was delighted.

"That's much better," said the King. "Now I can read my book properly."

"Here's your lamp back, genie," said William. "Now everyone is happy!"

The genie slid back into his lamp.
"Goodbye – and thank you," he called out happily, as he disappeared.

William was soon tucked up in his own bed again. "Magic lamps are all very well," he thought. "But they're not as good as wish wellingtons!"

Also available from BBC Children's Books:

William and the Dog
William and the Dinosaur
William in Space
Pirate William
Shrinking William

Published by BBC Children's Books
a division of BBC Worldwide Publishing Ltd
Woodlands, 80 Wood Lane, London W12 0TT
First published 1996
Text and illustrations © copyright BBC Children's Books 1996
Illustrations by Atholl McDonald.
From the television series by Hibbert Ralph Entertainment Limited
which is based on an original idea by Carole Lapworth
and original artwork by Vanessa Wild.

ISBN 0 563 38002 0

Typeset in Poppl-Pontifex by BBC Children's Books
Colour separations by DOT Gradations, Chelmsford

Printed and bound in Great Britain
by Cambus Litho, East Kilbride